MYSTERIOUS TALES OF JAPAN

MYSTERIOUS TALES OF JAPAN

RAFE MARTIN

ILLUSTRATED BY

TATSURO KIUCHI

G. P. PUTNAM'S SONS • NEW YORK

To the mysterious affinities that connect us all—
and for my mother, Sonia Martin

R.M.

To my grandparents

T.K.

Library of Congress Cataloging-in-Publication Data
Mysterious Tales of Japan / by Rafe Martin.   p.   cm.   Translation of folk tales of Japan.
Includes bibliographical references. Contents: Urashima Taro—Green willow—Ho-ichi the earless—
The snow woman—Kogi—The crane maiden—The pine of Akoya—Snake husband ; Frog friend—
The boy who drew cats—Black hair.   1. Fairy tales—Japan. 2. Tales—Japan.   [1. Fairy tales.
2. Folklore—Japan.]   I. Martin, Rafe, 1946–   . PZ8.M985   1996   398.2'0952—dc20
94-43464   CIP   AC   ISBN 0-399-22677-X   10 9 8 7 6 5 4 3 2 1 First Impression

CONTENTS

INTRODUCTION

It is for you, traveler,
To say how much is illusion.
—from *Nishikigi,* a Noh play

W<small>HEN I WAS GROWING UP</small> in New York City, our home was decorated with carvings, scrolls, paintings, clothing, and furniture from Asia. My mother especially loved things from China and Japan. My father, as an officer in intelligence and rescue for the Army Air Force in World War II, had been in China, Burma, and India. When he returned, he brought many beautiful objects, as well as photographs and stories. I grew up with these, and my imagination was absorbed not just with European fairy tales, Bible stories, family stories, legends of King Arthur, tales of Mowgli and Robin Hood, but with tales, peoples, and places of Asia too.

As I got older I learned more about Japan and its culture. I traveled there and discovered that the culture retains, even today, a fundamental respect for the Invisible. In a Shinto shrine you may see a stone on a brocade cushion with offerings of incense, tea, or flowers set before it. You may notice also certain old trees with rice-straw girdles knotted around their trunks—a sign of the indwelling of Spirit. On many street corners in the city of Kyoto, large, almost childish-looking carved stone figures of the

Bodhisattva Jizo, protector of children, travelers, and those lost at cross-roads—or in hells—sit protectively in full lotus position. Flowers and incense have been placed before these figures. Traffic whizzes by; shoppers stroll.

Shinto, the original religion of Japan, maintains that clouds, mountains, rocks, ponds, trees, and animals all have Spirit, or *kami* power. Nature is a vast, shimmering web of interconnecting beings and realms, a place of spiritual mystery and not a set of mechanisms. Buddhism, specifically Zen Buddhism, which has had a lasting effect on Japanese thought, aesthetics, martial arts, and religion, emphasizes that all forms of life are One and yet, simultaneously, each bug, leaf, mountain, person, dog, rock, or star is completely itself and unique. Compassion for every living thing permeates the Buddhist vision of reality.

These two cultural strands—Shinto and Buddhism—come together in the stories of Japan. In these tales we discover a universe filled with subtlety, mystery, inner power (concentrated spirit or, as the West has it, "virtù"), moral significance, and a deep sensitivity to the beauties of the natural world. Indeed, beauty itself may be a goal in these stories and it can be haunting. Cannot a phrase of poetry, a line of music, a gesture, the turn of a leaf, the fall of a wave, a face half seen haunt us, sometimes for years? The tales of Japan carry with them a special awareness of the fleeting yet haunting beauty we know from life.

Some of the most spiritual Japanese tales, for instance those drama-tized in the Noh theater, are ghost tales. But unlike many ghost stories familiar to Westerners, their purpose is not to horrify. Instead, they distill the essence of what is mysterious in life in order to remind us of the dreamlike—"ghostly," if you will—reality of all things.

Many of the stories in this collection owe their greatest debt to Lafcadio Hearn, an American writer who went to Japan in 1890, and remained there for the rest of his life. Hearn married a Japanese woman and, in time, began collecting traditional tales. He loved eerie ones. Hearn's work was based on old literary collections, on the writings of Zen, on Buddhist and Shinto sources, and on the versions of stories told to him by his Japanese wife and friends.

When I was presenting some of these stories several years ago in a Tokyo high school, a student explained that ghost tales, of which there are several in this collection, were traditionally recounted on summer nights. "Why?" I asked. "Because," she answered, "summer nights here in Japan are very muggy and very hot. Ghost tales make you shiver. They give you the chills." "Ah," I said. "So ghost tales are our original air-conditioning!" We may have laughed at that idea, but I think it is true that these tales can be a refreshing and much-needed breeze for our overheated and over-stimulated imaginations. I turn to them often, both to read for my own pleasure and to share with others. Their cool beauty never fails to restore my own imagination and the imaginations of my listeners. If the vigorously active, heroic fairy tales of the West display a sunlike immediacy and heat, the tales of Japan carry within them more of the moon's mysterious glow. May you enjoy your walk in the moonlight of imagination, then, with *Mysterious Tales of Japan.*

—Rafe Martin

URASHIMA TARO

It is deep midnight:
The River of Heaven
has changed its place.
—*Ransetsu*

ONCE THERE WAS A POOR but kindhearted fisherman named Urashima Taro. One day as he was walking along the beach, his nets rolled up on his shoulders, he passed some boys throwing sticks and stones at something crawling in the sand. What could it be?

He went over and saw a gigantic sea turtle that had crawled up out of the sea and was now trying to make its way back to the waves.

"Stop, boys!" he called. "Stop! Don't you know that every living thing on this earth is your brother or sister, and you should be kind? What's more, the turtle, the messenger of the Dragon King who lives under the sea, is said to live ten thousand years. If you kill something that might have lived ten thousand years, the loss of all those years will pile up on your own heads. It's dangerous and it's wrong. Here, boys," he said, digging into a little pouch that hung by his side, "take these coins and let the turtle go."

The boys took the coins. They let the turtle go. It crawled down the beach, entered the water, swam out into the waves, and then, just before diving down under the green sea, turned back and looked at Urashima Taro as if fixing his image in its mind. Then it dove down under the green sea, a thin stream of silver bubbles trailing behind, and was gone.

Urashima Taro went down the beach and put his nets into his boat. He pushed the boat out through the waves, jumped in, took up his oars, and began to row. He rowed and he rowed and he rowed.

Out on the sea the little boat rocked back and forth on the waves like a cradle. The sun shone brightly overhead, and the green sea sparkled below. Water slowly dripped, dripped, dripped from his oars and, as Urashima Taro sat in his little boat rocking gently, he began to feel sleepy. Before he knew what he was doing, he had put his head down on the side of that little boat and fallen asleep.

He had a dream. In this dream it seemed that a beautiful woman rose up out of the sea and began walking along the tops of the splashing waves without sinking into the sea at all. She walked straight toward his boat. Her long black hair hung down behind her. Her robe was crimson and blue. At her wrist and at her throat she wore pearls and corals and emeralds. And she was beautiful.

On she came across the water, closer and closer. She stepped into his boat, reached down and touched him on the shoulder, and . . .

Urashima Taro awoke. And there she was, just the way he had seen her in his dream!

"Who are you?" he stammered. "What do you want?"

She answered him in a voice both eerie and thrilling, a voice that murmured like the sea, "Urashima Taro, Urashima Taro, I am the daughter of the Dragon King from under the sea. And because of your kind deed to my father's messenger, the turtle, he has sent me to you to be your bride. We shall live together on the Island Where Summer Never Dies, if you wish."

Urashima Taro did wish. So she sat down beside him and took up one oar and he took up the other. And they began to row together. They rowed and they rowed and they rowed. And as the islands of Japan sank farther down into the sea, like a dream, up before them rose the Island Where Summer Never Dies. They rowed right through the surf. Urashima Taro jumped out and pulled the boat up onto the sand. Then he helped the princess step out upon the shore. But when he turned, what was this? There stood strange undersea creatures with crowns on their heads and robes on their bodies, saying, "Welcome, welcome kind Urashima Taro." And there on the beach Urashima Taro married the princess from under the sea.

Every day some new wonder was brought to entertain him. Sometimes it would be a pearl, but a pearl bigger than any ever seen, a pearl as big as a man's head. And the light shining from that pearl would be so bright that it could illumine a whole chamber of the palace. Sometimes giant sea serpents would coil around the stairwells of the palace. Then the light shining from their bodies would make it seem as if the stars had come down from the night sky. Sometimes an octopus or a squid would follow behind him the way a dog or cat might follow a person.

And for three years Urashima Taro was happy.

Then one day in the third year it was as if he suddenly awoke from a dream. "My mother," he said, "my father, my family, and friends. They must think I'm dead. I must go home for a short while and see them. I went out into the sea three years ago and never returned. How could I have done such a thing? And I miss them. I must return home and let them know that I am all right."

He went to his wife. "My mother, my father, my family, and friends," he said. "I left three years ago and never returned. They must think I'm dead. I must go home for a short while."

But she said in a voice that murmured like the sea, "Urashima Taro, Urashima Taro, don't go. If you go you will never return."

"Of course I will return," he insisted. "I would never leave you. I must go just to let my family and friends know that I am alive. I must see them one more time and make a proper farewell."

But once again she said, "Urashima Taro, Urashima Taro, don't go! If you go, I will never see you again."

"Do not fear," was all he said. "I will be back soon."

When she saw that he was going to go whether she wanted him to or not, she turned, reached back, and gave him a little black-lacquered wooden box tied with a silken cord. "Take this box and keep it with you always," she said in a voice as quiet as the softest lapping of a summer's sea. "It will help you come back to me. BUT!" And for an instant her voice was as strong as the breaking of a great, thundering wave. "You must never open the box! Do you understand?"

"I will keep it with me always and I will never open the box," he answered.

Then he ran down to his boat, put the box under the seat, and pushed out through the waves. He jumped in, took up his oars, and began to row. He rowed and he rowed and he rowed. And as he rowed the Island Where Summer Never Dies sank down into the sea, and up before him once again, like a dream, rose the island of his home, Japan.

He rowed through the surf, jumped out, and pulled the boat up on the sand so it wouldn't drift away. He lifted out the box and started up the beach. But what was this? Something was strange. When he had left, only three years before, the mountainside behind the village had been covered with trees. And now it was just bare rock. When he had left, only three years before, the trees of the grove had been tall and straight, yet now they were all twisted and bent. The houses were strange. He had never seen houses quite like that before. The people's clothing was strange, like none he had ever seen. Holding that box he walked up into the village. But the people's faces were strange to him too. This was his own home, his own village. Yet he didn't recognize a single soul.

What's going on? Urashima Taro wondered. *Why does everything seem so different? I'm going to go home.* But when he got to where his house should have been, no house stood there at all.

"What kind of strange illusion is this?" said Urashima Taro, confused.

Just then an old man came hobbling down the lane, leaning on a stick. "Old man," called out Urashima Taro, "old man, please help me."

"What do you want?" asked the old man.

"Help me, please, to find the house of one named Urashima Taro. He grew up here. He lived here. His mother and father live here still."

"Urashima Taro?" the old man said, scratching his beard. "Urashima Taro? Never heard of him." And he started off.

"Old man, wait, wait!" Urashima Taro cried. "I know he lives here. Please old one, think hard. Urashima Taro, Urashima Taro . . ."

"Urashima Taro?" the old man repeated once more. "Urashima Taro? Urashima Taro!" he suddenly exclaimed. "Why, my father's father told him the story of Urashima Taro, a young fisherman who went out into the sea one bright, sunlit, summer's day, three hundred years ago, and never returned. Urashima Taro! You want his home? It's the graveyard. You'll find his whole family there! But let me be!" And the old man hurried off.

"What kind of nightmare is this?" Urashima Taro said. Still carrying the box, he hurried to the graveyard, and there, in the oldest portion of the graveyard, under a great tree laden with moss, he found three large gravestones. They had been there for a long time, for they were all weathered, cracked, and split from many long years of summer's heat and winter's cold. And they were covered with thick, green, velvety moss.

Urashima Taro went up to the first stone and rubbed off the moss. And there, beneath the moss, carved in the stone, he read his mother's name. He went to the second stone, rubbed off the moss, and read his father's name. He went to the third stone, rubbed off the moss, and there was his own name. Overwhelmed, but still holding the box, he turned and wandered in a daze back down to the sea.

When he got there he stood on the sand as the waves rolled in and

rolled out around his feet. Finally he said aloud, "The secret of this nightmare, of this delusion, lies in this box. I must open the box and find out what's going on."

He untied the silken cord and dropped it onto the wet sand. He put one hand on the top of the box, took a deep breath, lifted up the lid, and *whoooossshhhh!* A thin white mist rose up out of the box and blew away across the ocean toward the Island Where Summer Never Dies.

All at once Urashima Taro felt old, tired, and weak. His hands shook and shriveled up before his eyes. His teeth loosened in their sockets and fell out. His hair turned gray, then white. Two tears dropped from his eyes and fell into the sea. And Urashima Taro, three hundred years old, collapsed onto the sand, turned to dust, and blew away across the ocean toward the Island Where Summer Never Dies.

If you ever travel to Japan, go to that village. Find the temple which still stands there. You'll see that inside that temple they keep the lacquered box, the cord it was tied with, and a piece of rope from Urashima Taro's boat, in memory of his story.

GREEN WILLOW

The moon in the water;
Broken again and again,
Still it is there.

—*Choshu*

Once there lived a young samurai named Tomotada.

Though he had been trained for war and was skilled in handling the bow, spear, and sword, he spent much of his time tending the trees of the palace grounds. Tomotada loved all green, growing things. But he greatly loved trees.

One day Tomotada was entrusted with an important mission. He was to carry a message scroll from his lord to the lord whose castle lay beyond the mountains. It was a great honor.

It was early autumn, the day bright and clear, when he rode out of the palace gates. The golden willow leaves waved in the breeze as if in farewell.

12

Tomotada rode all through that day. As he approached the mountains, the sky grew black. Lightning flashed, a cold wind blew, and a heavy rain was soon pelting down. Tomotada rode on, urging his horse forward along the slippery trails. Night was fast approaching. A fall on those mountain passes could easily mean death. Up ahead Tomotada saw a gleam of light. It vanished, then shone again. Heading toward it, he came to a small hut. Near the hut, by the banks of a stream, stood three willow trees. Two of the willows were old, heavy-limbed, and grew close together. The third willow was young, graceful, and slender. Willow branches tossed by the wind had hidden and then revealed the light shining through a crack in the hut's shuttered window.

Soaked and chilled, Tomotada tied his horse's reins to a willow and knocked at the door. It opened. "Come in, young sir," said the old man who stood in the doorway. "Come in out of the storm. Green Willow will see to your horse." Tomotada turned and saw a cloaked figure leading his horse to shelter. He stepped inside.

A hot bath took the chill from his bones. Dressed in dry clothes, Tomotada sat down to a steaming meal prepared by the old man's wife. The door opened and a cold wet wind blew in.

"My daughter," said his host, "Green Willow." Shyly the figure removed the wet cloak. Tomotada's heart skipped. The girl was beautiful, graceful as her namesake, the willow. Tomotada forgot his dinner. He forgot his mission. He could think only of Green Willow.

Late into the night Tomotada sat and talked with the old couple and with Green Willow. Green Willow's voice seemed as soft and sweet as the rustling of willow leaves to Tomotada. The turn of her neck, the lifting of her hands and arms were as graceful, as beautiful to him as the swaying of a young willow in a spring breeze.

At last Tomotada lay down to sleep. Outside, the wind moving through the leaves of the willow trees made a gentle music. Words for that music rose in his mind: "Green Willow. My wife will be Green Willow."

Alas for Tomotada, the next day dawned fair and clear. He would not be able to remain. Once more his mission called. With a heavy heart Tomotada watched as Green Willow led his horse from the stable. He saw the tears in her eyes. He knew then that he could never leave her. "I will be back," he said, "as soon as my duty is fulfilled." He mounted his horse and rode away.

All that day worry gnawed at his heart. Shouldn't he have asked for Green Willow's hand in marriage before he had left? Would he still find her there when he returned? Such thoughts gave him no peace.

As darkness fell he came to an abandoned temple. Wearily he dismounted. As he entered the temple, he heard a movement in the darkness. Instinctively drawing his sword, he called out, "Who is there? Show yourself or I strike." A figure rose from the shadows. "Green Willow!" And so it was. He sheathed his sword and held her close. How she had ever found him in that lonely spot, how she had arrived there before him—such thoughts he did not think. No. He had his Green Willow.

Tomotada could not leave Green Willow again. They set off along the roads together, little caring where those roads might lead. In time they came to a city where Tomotada's lord was unknown. They married and, with the money and jewels Tomotada carried sewn into the lining of his robe, they built a house near a stream. "Someday," he said, "I shall return to my lord and ask for his forgiveness. But not yet. No, I cannot leave yet."

Tomotada and Green Willow created a garden of many trees and flowers. Green Willow's love of trees and of green, growing things was as great as, if not greater than, Tomotada's own. They planted cherry trees and peach trees, pines and firs. And such flowers! Great blossomed peonies and chrysanthemums and tall irises all grew in profusion. And by the stream, there were willows. Tomotada and Green Willow were happy.

One summer's night Tomotada and Green Willow sat in their garden. Water splashed in the little stream nearby. Leaves rustled on the evening breeze. The perfume of many flowers scented the air. Suddenly Green Willow cried out in pain, "My tree! My tree!"

"What is it?" Tomotada asked urgently.

Perspiration stood on Green Willow's brow. "My tree!" she cried again. "My tree. Don't let them! Not now! Oh, but they are cutting, cutting. The pain! They are cutting my tree! Oh, dear Tomotada, husband," she said feverishly, "I am sorry that I took you from your duty. But I loved you. I shall always love you. Farewell."

"What are you saying?" he cried. "You are here with me. All is well. What . . . !" But before he could finish, Green Willow was gone! In his arms he held not a woman but a bunch of long, slender, golden willow leaves.

In his heart Tomotada knew the truth. But it was a truth that even he found hard to accept. He renounced the world, gave away all his possessions, and became a wandering monk, a disciple of the compassionate Buddha. Often he slept in the open fields beneath the stars or meditated alone in the mountains with only wild animals, rocks, and trees as companions. He prayed for all living things—animals, plants, and trees.

One day he found himself standing beside a familiar stream. It was, he realized with a start, the place where the hut had been when he had first met Green Willow. There were no traces of the hut at all. But three cutoff stumps remained standing there—all that was left of two old willows and a young one.

Putting his hands together, palm to palm, Tomotada sank to his knees and recited a prayer for the dead before the willow stumps.

Foolish man, he thought to himself, *what would people think to see you praying over willow stumps?*

Then hands still palm to palm, he once again chanted the words that bring peace to those gone beyond this earthly life.

Tomotada's pilgrimage was over. He built a hut on the spot, and there he remained. In the spring he discovered a green shoot growing from the stump of the young willow. Tomotada tended the shoot. It grew into a graceful sapling, which put forth slender leaves that rustled and whispered in the breeze. At night the music those leaves made moved through his dreams. "Green Willow," a voice sang to that music, "Green Willow."

The tree grew taller and more beautiful with each passing year.

At last Tomotada's life came to an end. A seed drifted down from the tree to rest where his bones had joined the earth. In time a new shoot came forth. The shoot grew and grew until it too was a sturdy tree. The trunks of the two willows grew together. The branches intertwined. Down under the earth the roots found each other in the darkness and embraced.

When the wind moves, rustling the leaves of those trees, it is as if they speak. "Tomotada," one tree seems to whisper, like a dreamer turning in sleep.

And the other seems to murmur as if in tender reply, "Green Willow, Green Willow."

HO·ICHI THE EARLESS

A famous moon!
Tonight the crabs even
Proclaim their Taira birth.
—*Issa*

FOR ALMOST ONE HUNDRED YEARS, the Heike family, also known as the Taira, ruled Japan with an iron fist. But after a time they grew complacent and no longer maintained the strength and vigor with which they had gained power. Another family, the Genji, began to challenge the Heike family for control. They fought terrible battles and finally, off the coast of Dan-no-ura, the two great clans faced each other in two fleets of ships for a confrontation.

As the ships sailed closer and closer, archers stood on the decks in their black armor, bowstrings drawn tight. Suddenly the air was filled with arrows. Men fell, pierced and screaming, into the sea. Ships crashed together, masts splintered and broke. Flames leapt everywhere.

The nursemaid of the baby emperor, seeing defeat all around her, took up the child emperor in her arms, walked to the prow of the ship, and, holding the royal child in her arms, leapt into the sea, her robes flapping around her. She and the child disappeared down into the bloody water and were never seen again.

The Heike family was destroyed, and after that, strange things began to happen along that coastline.

If ships tried to sail through those waters they'd be stopped, as if bony fingers were scraping along the bottoms of the hulls. Only with great effort could the oarsmen break away.

If swimmers were so foolish as to swim out from shore they were dragged down and never seen again. At night you had to be especially careful. Ghost fires would burn in the darkness. And if travelers were not wary they could be led by those ghostly lights to step off the cliff's edge and fall to the rocks below.

Even the crabs that crawled up out of the sea were strange. On their backs you could see a design in the shape of a helmeted face, the face of a dead samurai, impressed right in the shell.

By these signs the villagers who lived along that coast knew that the ghosts of the Heike had not found perfect peace. So they built a temple on the hillside over the sea, and behind the temple they built a graveyard. And in that graveyard they set up marker-stones inscribed with the names of each dead nobleman, noblewoman, and samurai. And they built a monument to the baby emperor and to his nursemaid who had carried him from defeat. They made offerings there. And things did quiet down. But strange things still sometimes happened.

One of the strangest involved a blind storyteller named Ho-ichi. He earned his living by going from town to town and accompanying himself on the *biwa,* an instrument like a lute or guitar. He would tell the story of the Heike and in this way he earned a little money or received food, clothing perhaps, and lodging for the night. It was a hard life for a blind man, traveling all alone.

The priest who was in charge of that temple off the coast of Dan-no ura loved stories. He heard of Ho-ichi's skill and invited him to his temple. "Ho-ichi," he said, "your life is hard; a blind man, traveling alone from town to town. Why not stay here? I love stories. All you'd have to do is tell me a tale now and then. Come, my friend, your life can be easier. In exchange for your stories I'll give you food, clothing, a place to live, and such money as you need. What do you say?"

So Ho-ichi settled down and his life was easier.

One hot summer's night the priest had to leave on some duty. Ho-ichi sat alone on the back deck of the temple. It was a hot, sticky night. Not a breath of air stirred the bushes. Sweat dripped slowly down Ho-ichi's neck into the collar of his robe. Off in the distance a bell struck midnight. *Bong!* The gate swung open—*creeeaak!* And heavy footsteps started down the path toward where Ho-ichi sat.

Ho-ichi could hear the sound of a sword hilt scraping armor and the scratching of the cords that tie on a samurai's helmet. He knew that it wasn't the priest returning, but a fully armed samurai coming toward him.

The footsteps came closer. They stopped just before Ho-ichi, and a voice like iron said, "HO-ICHI!"

"*Hai!* Yes!" Ho-ichi responded.

"Come with me," said the voice. "My lord, a lord of high degree, has heard of your skill in telling the story of the Heike clan, and now you must tell your tale to him. So rise and follow!"

Ho-ichi's heart beat with fear. He knew that to disobey the orders of a samurai could be fatal. Indeed, if a samurai did not like your response to a command, he might take out his sword and *sssssscccchhhhh!* Cut you in half!

"I'm blind," Ho-ichi stammered. "I cannot see to follow."

"Hmmm," said the voice, still gruff but more gently, "don't be afraid. Just raise your fist and I will guide you."

So Ho-ichi slung the cord of his *biwa* around his neck and raised his fist. Then a fist like an iron vise was clamped around his fist. He was raised to his feet and led off, down the path, through the yard of the temple, and out the gate, which swung closed behind him. He was guided down the narrow stone stairs that led to the village, through the twisting streets of the village, up a great hill, and then through a huge wooden gate that he did not remember ever having passed through before. They came to two huge barred wooden doors. The samurai pounded upon these doors with his mailed fist. "Open!" he called. "Open, for I have brought Ho-ichi!" The doors were unbarred and swung slowly open. Then Ho-ichi found himself being led into a huge room. Although he was blind he could hear very well. Voices murmured all around him in a refined and courtly tongue. He could hear the rustling of silken robes, and he knew that he was among a most wealthy and noble company. He was led to the center of the room. He kneeled on the mats and placed his *biwa* before him.

Then a woman's voice, rich and elegant, spoke, saying, "Welcome

Ho-ichi. We have heard of your skill in telling the tale of the Heike. Our lord, a lord of high degree, has therefore had you brought here so that you may tell your tale. Now you may begin.''

"Oh, Noble Host,'' Ho-ichi stammered, "the tale of the Heike is so long it takes four whole nights to tell. With which part of the story should I entertain this august company this evening?''

And the woman's voice said, ''Tell of the battle at Dan-no-ura, for the pain of that is most bitter—yet most sweet.'' As she said this there was something in her voice that chilled Ho-ichi's blood and made the hair prickle along his skull.

Then Ho-ichi took up his *biwa*. He strummed upon it and began to chant the story of the battle at Dan-no-ura. And as he did so, it seemed that once again the two fleets of ships faced one another. Once again the archers stood on the decks in their black armor. Once again the bowstrings were drawn tight. Once again the air was filled with arrows as men fell pierced and screaming into the sea. Again the ships crashed together, the masts splintered and broke, and flames leapt everywhere. Then the nursemaid of the baby emperor once more lifted the child up in her arms. She walked to the prow of the ship and, holding the child emperor in her arms, leapt into the sea, her robes flapping around her as she and the infant sank down under the bloody water.

As Ho-ichi played and as he chanted the tale, a wild sobbing, a wailing and crying, rose up around him, and he grew frightened. Never had any listeners responded so strongly to the tale. When he was done he could hear that noble company wiping their eyes on the sleeves of their silken robes. Then the woman's voice spoke again. ''Ho-ichi,'' she said, ''we had heard that you were a good storyteller, but we never knew how good. You must come again. Come three more nights and tell the whole tale. And," she added, "when you are done we shall reward you, greatly. BUT," she said, and there was again that something in her voice that chilled his blood, "you must tell no one where you have been! Is that understood?"

Ho-ichi's heart was pounding, but he thought to himself, *This is a noble, a wealthy company. If they like my work my fortune is assured.* And he cast aside his fear.

"Yes," he said, "I shall return. I will come three more nights and I will tell no one."

"Good. Now raise your fist. The samurai will guide you home. Remember, tell no one, Ho-ichi. And be ready tomorrow at midnight. Until then, farewell."

Once again Ho-ichi raised his fist. Once again a fist like an iron vise was clamped around his fist. Then he was guided to his feet and led out of the huge room. The wooden doors swung closed behind him. The bar was slid into place. Down the hill they went, through the narrow, twisting streets of the village and back up the stone stairs and into the temple yard. There the samurai left him, just as the sun was rising. Ho-ichi knew the dawn had come, for the birds were singing in the trees.

Ho-ichi stumbled to his quarters and slept all through the day, so exhausted was he. But that night, at midnight, he was ready. As the bell struck the hour, once again the samurai came for him and took him to the great palace on the hill. And there Ho-ichi told more of the tale and then returned at dawn, guided by the samurai. But that morning when he entered the temple, the priest was waiting.

"Ho-ichi, where have you been? A blind man out alone through the night. Tell me, my friend. What has happened?"

"It's a personal matter. A private affair. Don't be concerned. I am just very tired and must sleep." And stumbling past the priest, Ho-ichi went to his room, where he collapsed, completely exhausted, and fell at once into a deep sleep.

But the priest did worry. He knew that sometimes the ghosts of the Heike clan returned and did strange things. So that night he had two servants with covered lanterns in their hands waiting behind the low, stone wall that ran around the temple yard.

Just before midnight the two men saw Ho-ichi emerge from the temple and seat himself, legs folded beneath him, on the polished wooden deck at the rear of the temple. As the bell struck the hour, lightning flashed! Thunder crashed! Rain poured down. And the two servants, astonished, saw Ho-ichi sling his *biwa* on his back, raise his fist up into the night, and go running off into the darkness, alone!

They raised their lanterns and followed. But by the time they came to the village, Ho-ichi was gone. They had lost him. They knocked on many doors. But no one had seen Ho-ichi. They, with lanterns and eyes, had lost a blind man in a storm! How could it be? They were too ashamed to return and tell the priest. Instead, as the storm raged on, they continued their search for Ho-ichi.

It must have been about three in the morning when they heard a voice singing. They followed. It led to the graveyard. They peered over the wall. And there, seated in the pouring rain, splashed with the mud of the graves, was Ho-ichi playing upon the *biwa* and chanting the tale of the

Heike clan! And all around him, dancing and swaying and wavering to that music, were thousands upon thousands of the ghost fires!

The two servants were astonished. And they were scared. Still, they climbed over the low wall, crept up to Ho-ichi, and shook him. "Ho-ichi!" they cried. "Come with us! Come at once with us!"

But Ho-ichi was in some kind of trance. "What are you doing? Let me go! Don't embarrass me before this noble company!"

But the servants wouldn't release him. They held him tight, dragged him through the mud, carried him over the wall, and, teeth chattering with cold and fear, brought him back through the rain and the dark to the temple. There they put dry clothes upon him and gave him something hot to drink. Then the priest questioned Ho-ichi.

"Ho-ichi, what have you been doing? Where have you been going? You must tell me."

Then Ho-ichi, in great distress, told him the whole story. He said that he had been going up to a great palace or temple on a hill. And there he had been telling the story of the Heike clan to a most noble company. "One more night and I should have been greatly rewarded. But your servants have ruined it all. I am lost."

"No, Ho-ichi. No. Perhaps you are saved. For you see, you have not been telling your tale to the living but to the ghosts of the Heike clan themselves." Then he added even more gravely, "Alas, now that they know that you know who they are, when they come for you this night they will surely tear you to pieces. But they would have done something like that in any case. On this final night I am sure they planned to carry you off with them. Let me think. There must be some way. Hmmm. I have a plan.

Ho-ichi, you must be strong. You must be brave. And you must do just as I say. Now listen. I must leave the temple tonight, not to return until morning. It can't be helped. My servants, however, will paint sacred words over your body which will make you invisible to the ghosts. Then you must sit out alone again on the deck tonight. Only this night, when the ghosts come, do nothing. You must not rise or answer or respond in any way. Is that clear? No matter what they do, just sit unmoved, like a mountain. They will not be able to find you. Then they will leave and you will be free of them forever. But you must be strong and brave. I must leave now, my friend. I will be back in the morning. Farewell.''

The priest left. Then his attendants painted over Ho-ichi's body, even on his hands, palms, fingers, his shaven head, face, and eyelids, the words of a sacred text. They led Ho-ichi to the rear deck of the temple and they left him. They slid the door closed and locked it. And they hid themselves in the rooms farthest from the rear of the temple.

It was a hot, sticky night. Not a breath of air stirred the bushes. Sweat gathered under Ho-ichi's eyes. It dripped down his neck into the collar of his robe. Off in the distance a bell struck midnight. *Bonnggggg!* The gate swung open, *crreeeeeeaaak!* And heavy footsteps started down the path toward where Ho-ichi sat. They came closer, closer. He could hear the scraping and jangling of armor, the metallic clang as the sword hilt struck the samurai's mailed side. He could hear too the scratching of the cords that tied on the samurai's helmet.

And Ho-ichi's heart began to beat louder and louder. Then like a wave his fear rose up and broke completely over him. His whole body was shaking and his heart began pounding furiously. It seemed so loud now that to Ho-ichi it was as if a drum were pounding in the night. He was sure the ghost samurai would hear it and find him. But he could do nothing. He just sat there and sat there, the sweat pouring down his body and soaking his robe. Then the footsteps stopped just before Ho-ichi and a voice like iron said, "HO-ICHI!" But Ho-ichi said nothing. He just sat there and sat there. The footsteps walked all around him. At last they stopped right behind him. "Hmmm," said the voice, "I don't see this fellow. Where can he be? Still, I do see two ears. I will bring these ears back to my lord to prove I have done my job."

Then two fists, like iron vises, reached down, took hold of Ho-ichi's ears, and *rrrrrriiiiiiiippp!*

But Ho-ichi didn't cry out! He didn't move! He just sat there and sat there as the warm blood trickled down the sides of his face and soaked into his robe.

The iron footsteps marched off down the path. The gate swung closed. And once again the night was silent.

In the morning the priest returned with a covered lantern in his hand. As he walked along the stone path leading to the rear of the temple, he slipped in something wet. What could it be? He bent down, looked, and saw—blood! "Ho-ichi!" he cried as he hurried forward. "Ho-ichi!" There, on the rear deck of the temple, lay Ho-ichi, covered with blood, his hands pressed to the sides of his head. "Ho-ichi!" the priest cried. "Speak to me!"

When Ho-ichi heard the priest's voice, he sobbed out the whole story.

"It was my fault, my fault," exclaimed the priest in distress. "I should never have left. My servants made a terrible error. They forgot to paint

your ears. That is why the ghost warrior could see them. But oh, Ho-ichi, you were strong. You have come through the darkness with courage. You shall be free of these ghosts forever. Your life shall change. Come, let me bandage your wounds."

He took Ho-ichi into the temple and bandaged his wounds. In time those terrible wounds healed. When they did, once again Ho-ichi took up his *biwa* and began to play upon it. And once more he began to tell the story of the Heike clan. But now he also told of his own strange encounter with the ghosts of the Heike. Many great noblemen and samurai came to hear him so that, in time, he did become both rich and famous. But after this he was never known just as Ho-ichi again. He was always known as Ho-ichi the Earless.

THE SNOW WOMAN

In the icy moonlight
Small stones
Crunch underfoot.
—*Buson*

LONG AGO, A POOR WOODCUTTER and his mother lived in a little hut at the forest's edge.

Every day he went into the forest and chopped down dead trees. He'd lop off the dead branches, cut the wood to even lengths, and tie it into bundles. Then he would carry it back to the village to sell for firewood. In this way he supported his mother and himself.

One winter a bad storm buried the village in snow. The wood that could be cut near the village had already been taken. So when there was a lull in the storm, the young woodcutter set out into the forest with an old woodcutter from the village. They cut down a good-sized tree and

trimmed the branches. As they worked, snow began to fall. Quickly they
tied up the cut wood, hefted it onto their backs, and, bent under their
loads, headed for home.

The wind blew and the snow whirled around them. Great white flakes
blew against their eyes like feathers so that they could hardly see, and the
wind cut through their straw capes right to the bone. As they staggered on,
the drifts piled up around them. In no time the trails were completely
buried. The two men were lost and night was falling. They needed to find
shelter soon or they would die. They came to a river with ice floating in
the water. They would freeze if they tried to swim across. Then just ahead
along the shore, they saw an old, abandoned fisherman's hut. They stumbled in, exhausted, and propped the door closed behind them with a piece
of wood. But the hut was so old the wind just blew through the cracks in
the walls. They stacked the wood they had cut in a pile around their bodies
to keep that cold wind from them. At last, shivering and shaking in the
darkness, they drifted off to sleep.

Around midnight the young woodcutter awoke. The door of the hut
was open. The wind had stopped blowing. All was quiet and still. And
standing there in the moonlight was a beautiful woman. Her face, her
hands, and her robe were white as the snow, while her eyes and hair were
black as night. The young woodcutter thought he must be dreaming.

Then the woman glided silently forward. It was as if her feet were not
moving at all, or as if she had no feet. She approached the old woodcutter,
knelt beside him, and breathed upon him. Her breath was like smoke, and
as she breathed, the young woodcutter heard a sound like the whistling of
the snow-laden wind. *Whoooooowhhhhh.* And wherever that breath

touched, ice began to form. When she was done, the old man was frozen and dead.

Now the woman rose and glided toward the young woodcutter. She knelt beside him, bringing her pale, beautiful face closer and closer. The young man turned away. A tear trickled from his eye and ran down along his cheek. Then the pale woman smiled, and when she smiled the woodcutter could see her teeth. They were long and clear and pointed as icicles. In a voice soft as the falling snow, she said, "You are so young, so young. And so handsome. I shall spare you. BUT," she added, and the icy tone of her voice now made his blood freeze, "tell no one, not even your mother, of what you have seen this night. If you ever tell I shall instantly know of it. Then I shall return and make you wish that you had died this night with the old man there." Outside, the wind howled and the door pounded back and forth. She rose, glided silently over the floor, through the opened door, and was gone. The young woodcutter rushed to the door. He wedged it tightly closed again. Then he lay in the corner, shaking and shaking.

The villagers found him in the morning white with fear and the old man dead. They brought the young woodcutter back to the village, but he would not speak about the events of that night. And all that winter he refused to go back into those woods. But when spring came and the blossoms were forming, the leaves opening, the green grass growing, and the birds singing, the young woodcutter regained his courage. Once more he lifted up his ax and set out into the forest to cut down the dead trees, lop off the dead branches, and bring the wood home to support his mother and himself.

One spring evening as the young woodcutter was returning to his

village with a bundle of wood on his back, he met a young woman. She was pale, slender, and pretty. She told him that her parents had died and that now she was journeying to a distant city to find work with relatives there.

The young woodcutter said to her, "A young, attractive girl like you should not travel alone through this forest at night. There are robbers, bandits, rough, cruel men in these woods and . . . and worse. No. You must come back with me to the hut where I live with my old mother. You shall eat with us and spend the night in safety. Then in the morning, if you must go, you may walk through these woods when the sun is bright."

So she went with him. She said her name was Yuke, which means snow, and that she was grateful for his kindness. The woodcutter's old mother liked Yuke, and Yuke seemed completely at home in the little hut with the woodcutter and his mother. When the sun rose that morning, it was clear that she would not be leaving for she and the young woodcutter were already in love. Soon they married. In time they raised a family, two boys and a girl. When at last the old mother died, she died happily, for her life had been good. She had had a fine daughter-in-law and beautiful grandchildren. And the woodcutter? Why, he was happy too. His wife was indeed beautiful. And not just her face but even her heart and spirit seemed beautiful. And then too she seemed to stay as young-looking and as beautiful as the day he had first met her. Or so it seemed to him.

One winter's night near the New Year, the woodcutter and his wife sat together making gifts for the children. Though they had little money, their love was strong and they were capable people. What money could not provide they would make themselves. The woodcutter was weaving straw sandals for the children while his wife sewed little kimonos.

As Yuke sewed, the pale light from the oil lamp fell on her face.

Glancing at her for a moment, the woodcutter appeared startled. She smiled at him. "What is it, dear husband?"

"Oh," he said strangely, "I had forgotten."

"Forgotten what?" she asked.

"Once," he answered slowly, "years ago, maybe it was a dream, I cannot be sure now for it was so long ago—once I think I saw a woman as pale and as beautiful as you look in the lamplight now."

"Oh," his wife said, pausing in her sewing, "tell me about it."

And the woodcutter began to tell her of that night long ago when the woman of the snows had entered the hut, breathed upon the old man, and frozen him dead.

As he told the tale his wife sat up straighter. Though she continued her sewing, with his every word her face became more solemn and grave.

When he was done with the story, she had finished the last of the little robes. She bit the thread. Tenderly she placed the little kimono down upon the tatami matting beside the others she had already finished. She smoothed the little kimonos with a pale, graceful hand. Outside the wind began to blow. She rose to her feet. Her face turned white as the snows. Her hands turned white as the snows. Her robe too became all white.

She glided across the floor toward the woodcutter, who sat as if frozen, his eyes wide with disbelief and fear. "No dream!" she wailed. "It was I that night long ago. And I told you to tell no one! And now that you have told I should kill you most horribly, just as I promised. But no, I cannot. Ah, the pity of it! The spell is broken. I can no longer remain. Why did you speak? Because of this I must leave you, must leave my home and children." Turning toward the room where the children slept, she whispered as the wind continued to rise outside, "Be well, my dear little ones. I shall always watch over you." Then looking at the woodcutter, she hissed in a voice like blowing snow, "But I warn you. Care for our children well! For if I ever learn that you have harmed so much as a single hair of their heads, I shall return and do as I promised."

She glided soundlessly toward the door. Outside the wind howled. The door blew open and she glided through, rose up into the howling wind and storm, and was gone.

Now all that was long, long ago. Still, if you listen some winter's night as the wind comes moaning through the trees, you may hear a voice on the wind. It's the voice of the snow woman, yearning for her lost children and home.

KOGI

On the low-tide beach,
Everything we pick up
Moves.

—*Chiyo-ni*

O<small>NCE THERE WAS A PRIEST</small> named Kogi. He was fond of all living things, but fish evoked a special tenderness in his heart. Many people thought this odd. Fish are, after all, cold creatures. Still, even in Kogi's paintings of birds and flowers, a stream or a river or a lake was sure to appear. And if you looked carefully in the water of that stream or river or lake, you would find at least one fish.

To refine his paintings, Kogi made it a practice to go to the nearby lakeshore and pay fishermen to release their fish into a large tub where he would observe the fish carefully and sketch them. Their fluid motions and unceasing movement, their silvery scales and flowing fins captivated Kogi.

But after a time he began to feel their fear and their yearning to be free. So when he had painted or sketched the fish, he would put them back into the lake. Naturally, as a follower of the Buddha, Kogi ate no meat. But now he no longer ate fish. The very thought pained him.

One night Kogi lay down and fell at once into a profound sleep. He seemed to grow unbearably hot. Somehow he found himself by the lakeshore. The water looked so cool and inviting he removed his robes and plunged in. It was wonderful to swim. After a time he noticed how effortlessly the fish swam through the water. Despite himself he began to envy them. He had always felt that fish, while beautiful, were lesser creatures and that human beings were naturally superior. But now he began to see that in their own element, a fish's freedom and ease might be greater than a human's.

After a time a great golden carp rose from the green depths of the lake. "Friend Kogi," the great carp said, "you have shown us many kindnesses. We would like to reward you. For three days you can be transformed and become a fish. Would you like this?"

"Very much," Kogi answered, anxious now to know the freedom of a fish in water.

"Wait here," the golden-scaled carp said. "I shall return." And with a swish of its tail and a turn of its flowing fins it descended once again, disappearing down into those mysterious green depths.

For a time Kogi floated idly. Then he looked beneath the surface. Far, far below, something small like a golden dot was rising rapidly through the green water. It grew steadily larger and larger as it rose until at last the great carp once more appeared before him, its golden scales shining in the sun.

"Priest Kogi," the carp said, "it has all been arranged. The Master of the Waters has agreed. For three days you will be one of us. But take one warning to heart. Indeed, you must promise that you will heed it."

"I shall do just as you say," Kogi assured the golden fish.

"Do not eat any food from a baited hook."

"No. Never," he reassured the great golden fish.

"Very well," the golden carp said. "For three days you will know your desire. Swim free, swim deep. Farewell, friend Kogi." And with a swirl of fins and a whirl of bubbles, the golden carp was gone.

No longer did Kogi need to rise to the surface to breathe. No longer did he flail and struggle through the waves. Instead, like an arrow he sped effortlessly wherever his heart chose. Down and down he plunged into the deepening darkness of the lake's depths, where golden cities of coral and jewels—or so it seemed to him—awaited. Perhaps those magnificent cities were just formations of stone draped with seaweed, but to Kogi, as a fish, they seemed glorious.

He swam to the surface and, during a storm, rode pounding swells in the blackness of the night. Lightning forked across the sky. Thunder rolled. Exhilarated, Kogi once more dove deep down to where all is calm and still.

At daylight Kogi swam along the shore. He saw the fishing boats at the piers. He saw merchant vessels and men busy loading and unloading cargo. He saw shopkeepers opening their stores in the narrow streets near the wharves. He saw workmen setting forth, children running and playing, mothers strolling. Later he watched picnickers in the park and saw ships hoisting anchor, raising sail and leaving port. At nightfall he watched as the moon slowly rose and the torches were lit, burning and smoking along the water's edge. He saw these things with new eyes. All seemed strange to him now, wonderful and new.

And so it went for two enchanted days and nights. On the third day Kogi found that he was growing hungry. After a time it seemed that in all his life he had never known such a driving hunger. Then as he swam on he grew aware of a delicious odor permeating the water. So wonderfully enticing was this smell he simply had to swim toward it. At last he came to a little hook drifting before him. A bit of food was wrapped around the hook. *I am a man,* Kogi thought, *and could never be caught by such a thing. What's more, I know this fisherman. It's Bunshi's hook. If somehow I should become caught I can simply tell him to release me.* So Kogi foolishly thought.

Compelled beyond all reason, Kogi now rose to the bait. He bit—and was caught! He tugged and thrashed. But the hook was set and he was pulled, dangling and in agony, from the water.

"Help, Bunshi!" he cried. "Set me free! It is I, Kogi, the priest." But Bunshi seemed to hear nothing. Instead he reached out like a giant, slipped Kogi from the hook, and dropped him into a basket. "A fine fish," Bunshi proclaimed, "though I have never seen a fish whose jaws moved so!"

Bunshi set off at a rapid stride and came to the palace of the vice-governor. By now Kogi could hardly breathe. His skin seemed to be on fire. Yet he saw and heard everything clearly.

Bunshi presented his catch to the cook, who proclaimed, "Yes, it's a beauty," and bought the fish. Then the cook carried Kogi—as a fish—

through the main room, where the vice-governor was cutting open a peach with a silver knife while his brothers played Go.

"Your dinner, my lords," he said, holding the great fish aloft. The brothers cheered. In the kitchen the cook set Kogi down on the chopping block. He lifted a knife. "No! No!" Kogi cried desperately. "I am Kogi, the priest. Do not . . . !" The knife descended. For an instant Kogi felt a great, searing pain. Then he knew no more.

Slowly Kogi opened his eyes. He was lying in his own bed. A monk of his temple was sitting beside him. "Master!" exclaimed the monk. "You live!"

"How long have I been here?" Kogi asked weakly.

"Three days, Master. You fell into a coma. We could not rouse you. Even your heartbeat was still. We all thought you were dead. But as a faint warmth could still be felt over your heart, your funeral was held off."

"I am grateful," Kogi said, sitting up, "for then I would be dead indeed and you would have missed hearing a most interesting story. Call the others and summon too Vice-Governor Taira and his brothers from nearby. You will find them playing Go and drinking tea. Bring their cook as well. And bring the fisherman Bunshi. What I have to say concerns them all."

When all had gathered, and tea was served, Kogi told them his strange story.

"Master!" Bunshi exclaimed in horror when Kogi told of his being caught. "It's true. The jaws of the large fish I caught this morning were moving. It seemed to me as if it were speaking. I noted that. But no sound came forth."

"You lifted me off the hook, did you not?" Kogi continued. "And you put me in a basket. Then you carried me to the house of Vice-Governor Taira."

"Yes, Master," Bunshi said, growing pale at the memory, "it is as you say."

"I could not breathe," Kogi said. "My skin burned and such a yearning for the cool water filled my mind as I shall never forget. The vice-governor's brothers were playing Go and drinking tea."

"Yes! That's right," said the vice-governor and his brothers.

"And you, Vice-Governor, were eating a peach, cutting it open with a silver knife. Your brothers cheered when the cook showed them the fish he had just bought for their dinner."

"Ah," the vice-governor said, "that is all quite true. But how could you know?"

"My friend, this is no mere fable. It is all true. I was there. I really was the big fish Bunshi sold to your cook. When Bunshi lifted me from the basket and showed me to you, me the fine fish, I saw."

"Oh, Master," Bunshi said, now weeping, "I sold you."

"Master," the cook said in terror, "I too saw the fish's jaws moving. It was a great fish, Master. It did look like it was trying to speak. But I heard no words. Please, Master, forgive me."

"Yes," Kogi said calmly, "I remember that too. I was crying out, 'Don't do it! Don't kill me! I am Kogi, the priest.' "

"Oh, Master, what shall I do? If what you say is true I have murdered a disciple of the Buddha—an unpardonable crime."

"Do not fear," Kogi said. "It is over. You could not know. No, how could you possibly know? Then the knife descended. I felt a terrible pain. The next thing I knew I awoke here. So, are the details of this story correct?''

''They are, Master,'' all agreed.

''Then,'' Kogi murmured quietly, almost as if to himself, ''it is as I said. It was no dream.''

The guests left, the vice-governor and his brothers swearing that the fish's body would be returned, uneaten, to the lake. Indeed, the next day a funeral service, officiated by Kogi himself, was held for the fish and its body was given back to the waves.

After that Kogi returned to his ordinary life and painted fish whenever time permitted.

His paintings had been great before. But now they were so lifelike people said that if one of Kogi's scrolls ever fell into the water, the painting of the fish on it would surely swim away.

In fact many years later, long after Kogi's death, a cart carrying his scrolls to a nearby temple happened to tip into the water. The fish paintings on those scrolls all suddenly swished their tails, turned their fins, and then did, indeed, slip off the paper and swim away.

So unfortunately all we can know of Kogi's miraculous skill must now be found in this story.

THE CRANE MAIDEN

A day of quiet gladness,
Mount Fuji is veiled
In misty rain.

—*Basho*

ONCE, LONG AGO, an old couple lived all alone near the edges of a marsh. They were hard-working but poor.

One day the man had been gathering marsh plants, cattails, and such for his wife to cook. As he walked back along the trail, he heard a sharp cry and the sounds of someone—or something—struggling. Parting the long grasses by the trail's edge, he walked carefully into the marsh. The sounds—a clacking and a flapping, whirring noise—came from up ahead. Frightened but still curious, he stepped forward and looked. There on the ground before him lay a great white crane. Its leg was trapped in a snare and it was flapping desperately about trying to get free. Its beak was clacking open and shut. Its eye was wild with pain and fear. Its wings were muddied. Never had the man seen such desperation in a wild creature. His heart was moved. Speaking soothingly he drew closer. Somehow the crane seemed to sense his intent and grew calm. Gentle and slow were the man's movements as he approached. Then, bending down, he loosened the snare from the crane's leg and backed away.

The crane stood up. Flexing its injured leg, it stood there gazing directly at the man. Then opening its wings, it flapped once, twice, lifted up off the muddy ground, and flew away.

The man stood gazing after the great white bird as it made its way across the sky. Tears came to his eyes with the beauty of it. "I must see this clearly, and remember it, every detail," he said to himself. "How my wife will enjoy hearing of this adventure. I shall weave every detail into words for her, so she too will see."

"You are late," his wife said when her husband returned. "I have been worried. Are you all right?"

"I am better than all right, dear wife. I have had an adventure. I have seen such a sight. Wait, let me remove my sandals and sit down. I shall tell you all."

Then he told her of his finding the trapped crane, of the bird's panic and pain, and of the great joy he felt as he watched the white bird fly away.

"Dear husband, I am so glad you helped that wild creature. Truly it must have been a wondrous sight to see the crane rise up from the muddied ground and soar into the heavens."

"It was. It was. I have told it to you as best I could. For when I saw it fly I knew it was a sight you would have loved. And I wanted to share it with you."

"Thank you, husband." Then she steamed the plants he had gathered and they ate their rice and drank their tea and, when it grew late and the moon rose up in the blackness and sailed across the night sky, they let the fire sink down and they slept.

The next morning they heard a knocking at the door. The woman opened the door and there stood a young girl.

"I am lost," she said. "May I come in?"

"Of course. Come in, dear child," the old woman said. "Have a cup of tea. Sit down."

So the girl came in. She was alone in this world, she said. "Let me confess," she added, after drinking the tea and eating the rice the old couple gave her, "I would like to stay here with you. I am a hard worker. I no longer wish to be alone. You are kind people. Please let me stay."

The old couple had always wanted a daughter, and so it was agreed.

"Thank you," the girl said. "I do not think you will regret it." She peered curiously around the house. She looked into an adjoining room. Her face lit up. "I see you have a loom. May I use it from time to time?"

"Daughter," the woman said, "all that we have is yours. Of course you may use the loom."

"I am a shy weaver," the girl said. "Please, Mother, please, Father, when I am weaving do not look into the room until I am done. Will you promise me this?"

"It will be as you wish, child."

The next day their new daughter said she would go into the weaving room. The door was to be shut and neither her father nor her mother were to look in until her work was completed.

All day the girl sat at the loom. And all day the old couple heard the clacking and the whirring of the shuttle, the spinning of the bobbins of thread.

When the sun was setting the girl emerged, pale and worn. But in her hands she held the most splendid cloth the old couple had ever seen. The pattern was perfect, the colors glowing. Images of the marsh, the sun, the flight of cranes flowed elegantly through the finely woven material.

"Mother, Father, please take this cloth to the market and sell it. With the money your life will become easier. I want to do this for you."

The old people were astonished at their daughter's skill. The next day the man brought the cloth to the town. Immediately people began to bid for the beautiful cloth, which was sold at last for three ryo of gold—an unheard of sum.

That night the old couple and their daughter, dressed in new kimonos, ate a wonderful meal—all bought with a small bit of the gold. For several months life was easy. But then the money was gone.

Once more the daughter entered the room, closed the door, and began to weave. *Clack clack clack, whirr whirr whirr.* Hours later she emerged, pale and worn. In her arms was a cloth that shone like silver, filled with patterns of the moon and stars, patterns of sunlight and moonlight shining on water. The old couple had never imagined a material of such stunning beauty.

But once again the girl said, "Mother, Father, do not keep the cloth. I can make more. Please sell it and use the money to care for your old age."

So again the man took the cloth to town. The merchants were astonished. They bid furiously, one against the other, until the cloth had been sold for six ryo of gold.

For many months the family lived happily together. But in time, that money too was gone. The daughter went once again to the loom. But this time her mother and father were curious. Why must they not look? They couldn't bear it. They decided that they would take just a peek through a crack in the wall. If their daughter could not see them, they reasoned, it would not disturb her at all.

Clack clack clack, whirr whirr whirr. The man and the woman walked softly along the wall, knelt down, and peered through a thin crack in the paper wall. At the loom sat a white crane pulling feathers from its own breast and wings with its long bill. It was weaving with those feathers. The crane turned toward the crack and looked with a great black mournful eye. The man and the woman tumbled backward. But it was too late. They had been seen.

Later, when the door of the room opened, their daughter emerged, pale and worn. In her arms she held a most magnificent cloth. On it were images of the setting sun, the rising moon, the trees in autumn, the long migrations of the cranes. On it too were the images of a man and a woman watching a white crane fly away.

"Father, Mother," she said, "I had hoped to stay with you always. But you have seen me as I truly am. I am the crane you saved, Father, from the trap. I wanted to repay you for your kindness. I shall never forget you, but now that you know this truth, I cannot stay with you."

The man and the woman wept. They begged and pleaded, "We love you. Do not leave us. We do not care that you are a crane! You are our daughter. We shall tell no one."

"It is too late," whispered the girl. "The marshes call to me. The sky calls to me. The wind in the trees whispers my name. And I must follow. Perhaps all is as it should be. The debt has been repaid. I shall never forget you. Farewell.''

She walked from the hut and stood out in the open air. The man and the woman watched in wonder as before their eyes their beautiful pale daughter became a beautiful white crane. Flapping her wings once, twice, three times, the great crane rose slowly up off the ground and, circling the hut, flew away.

''Farewell,'' said the man and the woman, watching the crane disappear over the marsh. ''We shall miss you, daughter. But we are glad that you are free.''

After that, every year when the cranes migrated, the old couple left a silver dish of grain out before their door. And every year a beautiful crane came to eat that grain.

So the story goes.

THE PINE OF AKOYA

I heard the unblown flute
In the deep tree shades
of the Temple of Suma
—*Basho*

MORE THAN A THOUSAND YEARS AGO, there lived a governor named Fujiwara Toyomitsu with his daughter, Akoya. Not only was she beautiful, but she was a talented and accomplished musician.

Each night, but especially when the moon was bright, Akoya loved to sit near the polished wooden deck, just inside the opened sliding *shoji* screens. Facing into the garden, she would play the stringed *koto*. The music floated up, each note resonant and still. It seemed to her, as she played, that the bushes and trees swayed, their leaves rustled and whispered in time to her music.

One night when her father was away and Akoya played her *koto* in the moonlight, someone began playing a flute nearby. The harmonies the flute made with the *koto* were exquisite. Akoya's heart beat with excitement and wonder. The music ended. All she heard was the wind moving through the trees. She hoped the flute player would appear. But no one did.

The next night Akoya played again. The night was calm and still, the moon's light still bright. She began to play and, as she played, her music seemed to clearly express her truest feelings—her love for the garden, her yearnings for true friendship, the sadness she still felt over her mother's death two years before. The clouds, the moon, the flowers, and trees all seemed to listen. Then from the velvety darkness arose once more the notes of the mysterious flute. Its eerie, tender notes matched her music perfectly. Flute and *koto* soared and harmonized. Akoya's loneliness left her completely.

When the music ended she waited expectantly. "Please," she said, "won't you step from the shadows? Let us meet."

A young man wearing a green robe stepped from beneath the trees. In his hand was a silver flute. "My name is Natori Taro. I live alone at the foot of Chitose Mountain. I was traveling through these parts when I heard of you and your music. Several nights ago I came to listen and was entranced. Never had I heard such beautiful music! I longed to play along with you. Last night I had the courage to do so."

"You are too kind," murmured Akoya.

Natori came closer. He lifted his flute and began to play. Akoya plucked the strings of the *koto*. Music of such haunting beauty filled the garden that the trees and bushes seemed to sway to it. The twinkling stars and wandering clouds seemed to move in rhythm to it. The night flew by and then, just before the dawn, Natori ceased. "Dear Akoya, now I must leave."

Akoya paled. "But you will return?" she asked, her heart skipping, losing its rhythm.

"If you wish it," Natori answered quietly.

And Akoya said, "Yes."

And so he returned the next night. Once more their music filled the garden. And their love grew. It grew and grew. And Akoya was happy.

One night, as the moon's light was fading, Natori, seated beside Akoya, spoke. And his voice this night was filled with sorrow. "Dear Akoya, I cannot stay with you. It is not because I wish to leave, and there is no other who has a place in my heart. I must return home because I have agreed to help my people. And when I return, I shall die."

Akoya gasped, but Natori went on, "My days here with you have been the happiest of my life. Our music will not end. Do not doubt me. Come to the foot of Chitose Mountain and you will know the truth of my words."

Then Natori rose and quickly stepped through the open *shoji.* As he passed along the paper wall, he cast a shadow in the torchlight. Akoya gasped. The shadow was not that of a man but of a pine tree.

Akoya ran out. The torches smoked and flared but there was no sign of Natori. From off in the distance came the sound of his silver flute, so beautiful and haunting. The notes trailed off and were gone.

Several days later Akoya's father returned. "Daughter, a strange thing has happened at Chitose Mountain."

When Akoya heard that name her heart began to beat very fast. "What is it?" she managed to ask.

"As you know the famous wooden bridge over the Natori River was damaged this spring in the floods. It must be repaired soon or it may collapse. A great pine tree was found growing at the foot of Chitose Mountain, not far from the river. Huge, straight, and solid, it will provide the perfect log to repair the bridge. So I gave the order for it to be cut."

"Yes, Father," Akoya stammered, "go on."

"The tree was felled and the branches cut away. But it is so huge and heavy that a hundred men have been tugging at the log and it will not budge. I am sending more men and will go back myself in another day to oversee the work. Imagine! One hundred men and still the log cannot be moved! Not even an inch. No one has ever seen such a thing."

"Take me with you, Father," Akoya said.

They left the next day, and after several days traveling, arrived at the foot of Chitose Mountain. The great pine lay where it had fallen. Many hundreds of people—in addition to the hundreds of workmen sent by Akoya's father—had gathered there. Men, women, and children; lords and noblewomen, samurai, peasants, and working people—all had come to see the great log that could not be moved. It was like a holiday.

Akoya approached and ran her hands along the log. It seemed to shiver.

"Do you see! Do you see that!" cried the people. "The log moved!"

Akoya seemed to hear the music of a silver flute. "I am here, Natori," she said quietly, "and I do not doubt you."

She bent down, reached her arms around the log, and lifted it up. The

crowd surged around her, and hundreds of hands took hold. They carried the log to the river and set it in the water. The great log floated easily. "We can float it to the bridge now," the workmen said. "The bridge will be repaired. It is a miracle."

Akoya sat where the log had lain. Its shape showed as a great hollow pressed into the earth and bent grasses. There, in the hollow, lay Natori's silver flute. Cut into its surface, the way the names of lovers are cut into the bark of a tree, were the names *Akoya* and *Natori*.

Akoya kept the flute beside her always. Generations passed. In time another great pine grew at the foot of Chitose Mountain. It is known, even today, as the Pine of Akoya.

A FROG'S GIFT

In the summer rains
The frogs are swimming
At the very door.

—*Sampu*

ONCE A FARMER WALKING ALONG THE ROAD passed a field and saw a snake about to eat a frog. Without thinking he exclaimed, "Stop, Snake! Please let the frog go."

The snake turned toward him, its eyes glittering. "Why?" hissed the snake. "Will you take the frog's place?" And it opened its jaws wide and gave another long and horrible hiss.

"No," stammered the farmer, frozen with fear. "No. But I'll . . . I'll give you one of my daughters to marry." The snake's eyes glittered more brightly yet. "Done!" hissed the snake. And it closed its jaws with a snap.

At once the frog hopped into the water of the rice paddy and, *splash*, it was gone. The snake too glided quickly away. Ripples spread on the surface of the water, and as the farmer watched them fade, he began to wonder, with some dread, about what he had done.

When he reached home he went to his oldest daughter and said, "To free another creature I have promised a daughter to a snake. Will you go?"

"Never, Father!" she screamed. "How could you!"

He went to his second daughter. "I have offered one of my daughters to be a snake's bride. I saw a frog about to be eaten. This was the only way to save it—unless I let the snake devour me! Will you do it?"

"I won't!" shouted the second daughter. "Marry a snake! You must be mad!"

He went to his third and youngest daughter, but he didn't have much hope. "I have done a foolish thing," he said.

"What, Father?" his daughter asked.

"I saw a snake about to devour a frog," he answered, "and I felt so sorry for it that I found myself offering a daughter to save this frog. So, my daughter, will you marry the snake?"

"I will, Father," the third daughter answered. "It was a kind thing you did. But you must bring me one thousand gourds and one thousand needles before I will go."

"I will have them ready in the morning," the farmer promised. "And, Daughter, thank you."

The next morning the farmer went to town. He bought one thousand gourds and one thousand needles and hurried home.

Toward twilight the farmer and his daughters heard a drum beating. They looked down the road and saw a great host of armed men coming toward them. The torches they carried made their armor glitter and shine like scales. In the middle of this company of one thousand armed men rode a mighty warrior on horseback.

"I have come," said this handsome warrior in a low, hissing voice, "for the girl."

Weeping, the farmer packed the gourds and the needles. Then as the sun went down the poor girl set off with the great host of men into the blackness of the night.

They journeyed for several hours. They came at last to a great shining palace enclosed by a high wall of stone. The gates opened and the host passed within. But what was this? Once within the gates, the men turned into snakes. Their eyes glittered. Their scales shone. Their tongues flicked in and out. And they began to writhe and dance, turning and twisting in the dust. They seemed hungry and the girl began to fear that it was not a wedding but a feast to which she had been brought. And that she herself would be the meal. Then the Snake Lord said, "Sweet is this girl, sweeter than frogs!" and the others laughed and hissed.

Then the girl said, "I am ready for whatever may come. But before that I have one request. I must know your worth. I have a simple test. Sink one thousand gourds; float one thousand needles."

"That'sssssss eassssy," hissed the snakes. "Give us each a gourd and a needle and it will be done."

So the girl opened her pack and the snakes began trying to sink the gourds and float the needles. But gourds being hollow and light can only float, and needles being solid iron will only sink.

The snakes were becoming exhausted—and furious—as their efforts

failed. The chaos and the din grew louder and louder. In the midst of the confusion the girl ran. She opened the gate a crack, slipped through, and went running, running out into the darkness. In time she came to a little hut in the marshes. A fire was burning within. Exhausted, she knocked on the door. An old woman in a green robe with dark spots printed on it opened the door. She was small and squat but her wide eyes seemed kind. "Come in, dear," she croaked. "The smoke has made my voice hoarse, but you will be warm and safe here. Appearances are often deceptive. But I promise no harm shall come to you. Come in." The girl entered and the old woman closed the door tightly behind her.

"First eat," the old woman said in that strange, hoarse voice, "then we shall talk."

She brought the girl hot food and tea, rice, and many good things, and the girl ate and ate.

"Tell me your troubles, dear. Perhaps I can help."

The girl told the old woman all that had happened. The old woman didn't seem scared or amazed at all. She just chuckled. "A thousand gourds to sink, a thousand needles to float. Oh, that's a good one. Yes, yes. That was good thinking indeed.

"Rest now, little daughter, and in the morning I'm sure I'll be able to help you find your way."

The girl was so tired she fell asleep almost at once. As she drifted off she heard frogs croaking melodiously from the marsh, and somehow it sounded beautiful.

In the morning the old woman prepared fresh tea. Then she told the girl, "I have thought about you a lot, my dear. And I have made inquiries on your behalf. My friends have told me that the lord of all this land is looking for a bride. You are beautiful, kind, and openhearted. I am sure it is you he seeks. I have a new kimono for you. It is fine, is it not?" And she held up a light green kimono beautifully made and splashed handsomely with the greens and yellows of the rice fields. It was indeed a beautiful thing. "Put this on and we shall go to the town."

When they arrived at the town, hundreds of girls were already waiting by the castle. The old woman led the girl to the end of the line. The steward came along, looking at each girl. "Maybe," he would say. Or, "No." When he got to the old woman and the girl, he smiled. "This is the one," he announced. "I'm sure of it. You may all go home. This girl shall be our dear lord's bride."

The old woman smiled a great *wide* smile. She blinked her large round eyes. She bowed. "Good-bye, dear child," she croaked. Then she turned and walked away with a hop to her step.

The girl was married to the great lord. They lived happily. Her father and sisters came to live nearby and were astonished that she who had been promised to a snake should have made such a good match in the end.

But she had, after all, saved the life of a frog. "And that might," said the girl, "have had quite a lot to do with it."

THE BOY WHO DREW CATS

Shutting the great temple gate,
Creak! it goes:
An autumn evening.

—*Shiki*

Many years ago, a boy lived on a farm with his mother, father, older brother, and sister. One fall, near harvest time, almost as if overnight, the earth dried up and crops withered. It was strange, said all the people, how quickly it happened. Many people in that province suffered and no matter how hard the boy and his family worked, they could not grow enough to eat.

One day the mother and father were forced to make a painful decision. They decided that they would bring their youngest son, who was the most delicate of their children, to a temple. Living there he would have food and shelter and so would survive. But it might mean they would never see him again.

With heavy hearts they set out. When they arrived the abbot received them kindly. "Why have you come?" he asked.

"Please help us. We have so little food. We fear that our young son will not survive until the crops come in again. He is intelligent, bright, and quick. Please accept him as a novice and let him live here."

"We shall see," said the abbot. Then he asked the boy three questions. No one today knows what those questions were, but it's said that the boy answered them so quickly the abbot immediately said, "Yes, you can stay."

The parents left. For a long while the boy stood at the temple gate, waving in farewell. His parents, waving back, walked on. They seemed to grow smaller and smaller with the distance until, at last, the boy could see them no more. How alone he felt. He knew no one and all those around him were adults, strangers, who looked so grim. But the abbot told him, "You are a bright boy. Just do the job you are assigned and all will be well. That is our rule here. Outside our times of meditation and of sutra chanting, we work together at necessary tasks. Do you understand?"

"*Hai!*" said the boy. "Yes."

"Good," the abbot said. "Tomorrow we shall start you at a useful job."

The boy bowed to the abbot of the temple and left. He found a place to sleep on the tatami matting of the sleeping-hall floor. Then, unrolling his bedroll, he carefully placed his three most precious possessions, which he had kept safely tucked inside the rolled blanket, beside his pillow. These were a bamboo-handled brush with a fine tip of smooth bristles; a stick of compressed black ink, hard as wood; and a stone tray for mixing the

powdered ink with water so he might draw. The boy loved to draw. And what he loved drawing more than anything else was cats.

In the morning the boy arose and worked along with the monks doing the jobs he was given—sweeping leaves, cutting firewood, stoking the fire. The second day he again worked along with the others, and all was well.

The third day the monks and priests in that temple awoke, stretched, yaaaawwwned, put on their robes, went out into the central hall of the temple, and, "WHAT IS THIS?!" they cried. For there were cats drawn on the floors!

"Who is drawing cats here?" they exclaimed, and they observed the new boy carefully. But they could see nothing out of the ordinary. So they let it go by.

The next day the monks and priests in that temple awoke, put on their robes, went out into the central hall, and "WHAT IS THIS?!!!" they cried again. For now there were cats drawn on the walls!

"WHO IS DRAWING CATS?" they once more exclaimed. And again they watched the boy carefully. But again they saw nothing out of the ordinary, and again they let it go by.

The third day came. The monks and priests immediately rose. They yaaaaaaawwwned and stretcchhhed, put on their robes, and hurried out into the still-darkened central hall of the temple. They peered at the floors. But the floors seemed fine. They looked at the walls. The paper walls too were free of cats. They looked at the ceilings. . . . But the ceilings were also untouched. "So," they said with a sigh, "it's over." They took out their sutra books, opened them, and, "WHAT IS

THIS???!!!!!'' There were cats drawn on the blank pages and margins of the books!

Angrily they closed their books and stormed to the abbot's quarters. ''The new boy is drawing cats on everything! We are sure of it. Get him to stop or send him away.''

The head of the temple called the boy to him, and quietly asked, ''Are you the one who's drawing these cats?''

''Yes,'' he admitted, ''but I don't mean harm by it. I don't mean to destroy temple property or to ruin walls or floors or books. It's just that I see a clear stretch of flooring or wall or a clear page in a book, and I SEE cats. It's as if they spring up out of me. Then before I know what I'm doing, I've ground up my ink, taken out my brush, and drawn my cats. Please understand.''

''Perhaps you are destined to be an artist,'' said the priest, ''Still, here you must do the job you have been assigned. It is our way. If you cannot then you will have to leave. Do your best. I give you one more chance.''

The boy knew it might mean his death to leave the temple with the drought still on. There was so little food anywhere and he was a long way from home. He made up his mind to work hard. He would not draw cats.

The next day the boy arose with the others. He worked at the jobs he was assigned, and all went well. All was well too the second day.

On the third day he awoke, yawned, stretched, and then, before he knew quite what he was doing, suddenly ground up a bit of ink on the little stone tray, dipped in his wet brush, and drew a cat on the wall by his bed! The monks all saw it.

The abbot of the temple said to him, ''The signs are quite clear. Your destiny is calling. You must follow wherever it leads. Now listen carefully to what I say, for I'll give you a warning: Avoid large places. Stay in small places.''

The boy didn't know what was meant by this but, hoping things would become clearer as he went along, he responded, *''Hai.* Yes. Thank you, I will.'' Carefully rolling up his precious drawing things in his bedroll, he tied the cord around the bundle, threw it over his shoulder, and set out on the road alone.

It was late in the fall. The sky was low and gray and the wind came mooaaaning through the trees. The dead leaves rattled on the branches like bones, *chkk chkk chkk.* And the boy began to get scared. Where would he go? Where would he stay? Who would care for him? How would he eat? How would he live? Surely he would starve on the roads, or freeze! Then he remembered. Twelve miles away, on a hill, was a great temple, so big that perhaps they even needed an artist there and he might do what he loved doing most in this world—he might draw. But even if they didn't need an artist, he could cook or clean or chop wood. Whatever was needed, he decided, he would do it. And with this hope and determination in his heart, he set off for that other temple.

But what he didn't know was that the temple had been abandoned and that a goblin now lived there. At night when travelers went into that abandoned temple, lay down, and went to sleep, the goblin would creep out along the floors. And while they were sleeping it would gobble them up!

The boy knew nothing of this. As he walked along, the day got darker and darker and colder and colder. Then, just before nightfall, he came at last to the gate of the temple. He walked up to the great doors and knocked. *Boom! Boom! Boom!* Each knock rang out, echoing hollowly.

"How strange," he mused. "Someone should be here to open the door for travelers. It is the proper way. Ah, it must be because of the drought. They must all be out in the fields tending to the crops. When they return I will show them that I'm a willing worker. They can use my help here. I'll have a home. Still it is so dark and cold and I am so hungry and tired I had better go inside and wait."

He pushed on the door, *creeeeaaaaak!* "Such rusty hinges! Someone is supposed to have the job of polishing and oiling them. I can do this. When they return I'll show them I am ready to work and they will give me a home."

He pushed the door open, *creeeeaaaak!* and stepped inside. "OOOOHHH! WHAT IS THAT?!" Cobwebs hanging along the entrance-way had brushed his face in the darkness. "Ah, they must be so busy working in the fields that they no longer have the strength to do even these necessary jobs. I'll do this for them. When they return they will surely give me a home."

He found an old broom and swept up the area around the entrance-way. He coughed and choked and sneezed, it was so dusty, but after a while, the job was done.

But now it was late. The moon was high in the sky and still no one had returned. The moonlight shone faintly through the paper walls of the temple, casting strange shadows into the room. The boy was so tired. He had walked all day. He was cold. He had had nothing to eat. And he was somewhat scared, too. After all, where could they all be? It seemed too late for the monks still to be working in the fields.

The boy decided he could wait up no longer. "I must lie down and sleep," he said to himself. "Surely, when I awake in the morning the monks will be back and everything will be all right."

He untied the cord on his bedroll and unrolled the blanket. He put his three precious drawing things beside him, then, covering himself over, began to drift off to sleep—when he noticed something white and glimmering by his head. What could it be? He reached out and touched—a set of folding screens—frames of wood, hinged together to form three panels. The panels were covered with fine, smooth rice paper. The boy took one look at those screens and one thought came unbidden to his mind: CATS!

He ran to the front door and opened it. A little stream flowed through the dead leaves. He scooped up a palmful of cold water and poured it on his grinding stone. He ground up his ink, dipped in his brush, and drew—running cats, sitting cats, dancing cats, playing cats, fighting cats, meowing cats all over those screens until the screens were covered with cats. He stepped back and looked. "Oh," he exclaimed in satisfaction, "I have been drawing cats for a long time, but at last my cats have come out perfectly. They are just as I've always hoped they would be. Whatever happens now," he added, "I won't worry. My cats are here."

Washing out his brush, he once again lay down and started to drift off to sleep. All at once he remembered the words of the priest: "Avoid large places, stay in small places!" The boy looked around and saw that he was in a huge room, the kind of room he had been warned against.

"I must find a small place." He looked and looked, and then, behind the screens, found a little cupboard with a sliding paper-door front. "Here is a small place. I'll be safe here." And gathering his drawing things and blanket, he crept into that small place, slid the door closed, and, at last, exhausted, fell fast asleep.

Suddenly, in the middle of the night, a horrible screaming and howling filled the temple as walls were smashed, furniture broken. Then, finally, there was silence. All night long the little boy lay in that cupboard, shaking and shaking, not knowing what was waiting just outside that thin paper door.

In the morning the moon went down and the sun came up. The sun's light filtered through the paper walls of the temple. It filtered through the paper door of the little cupboard and the boy knew it was now or never. Either he had the courage to open the door and face what was there now or he'd never have the courage to do it and he would die in there.

He took his blanket and drawing things in one hand, then put his other hand on the door of the cupboard. Slowly he slid the door back just a bit and peered out. But he couldn't see anything, for he was behind the screens. Still gripping his blanket and drawing things in his hand, he slid the door back all the way, crept out, took a deep breath, stuck his head around the screens, and looked. It was horrible!

Blood was splattered on the walls and sprayed on the ceiling. And in the center of that room, in a sea of blood, was an immense rat-goblin—dead!

"Oh," exclaimed the little boy as his fear subsided and his relief and astonishment grew, "who was it who saved me from this horrible monster? Who was it who saved my life from this demon who had come in the night to tear me to pieces?"

Then he looked up at the screens where he had drawn those cats with so much love and care. And from every tooth and from every claw, blood was dripping down the screens. Those cats had come to life in the night. And it was those very cats who had saved him.

The boy returned to the first temple and told the abbot what had happened. The abbot understood the significance of the goblin's death. "The goblin was undoubtedly the cause of the famine. Now that it is dead all will be well. It seems you saved not only yourself with your art, but your family and the whole province as well. This is a high destiny indeed."

And it was so. That spring the fields were gloriously lush and green. It was the best harvest in years. The boy returned home. His parents were so happy to see him, and he was happy to see them.

In time the boy became a great artist known throughout the islands of Japan.

But it's said no matter how great he became, every day he took out his ink stick, poured water on his grinding stone, ground up his ink, dipped in his brush, and drew at least one cat.

BLACK HAIR

An autumn evening.
Without a cry,
A crow passes.
—*Kishu*

Long ago in the city of kyoto, there lived a samurai. He was married to a good and beautiful woman who was a fine weaver. For some reason this samurai lost his position. It may have been that his lord died. In any case he was now masterless, a *ronin*.

Though his wife sold the cloth she wove, they still fell into poor circumstances. It was not quite poverty but it was certainly no position of honor. The samurai was ashamed at this change of fortune. In time he grew resentful.

One day he tied up a bundle of belongings and girded on his swords. "I am leaving," he said to his wife. "This is no life for a grown man. I

cannot stand this disgrace. Marry another. I shall seek better fortune." She wept and pleaded. "I will weave more, sell more," she cried. "I'll work harder. Please, I beg you. Do not abandon me."

But it was no use. His heart was hardened. As she wept, her long black hair flowing over her shoulders, he tied on his sandals. As she sobbed, he mounted his horse and rode away.

He traveled to a distant city. In time he entered the service of another lord. Because his skills were impressive he swiftly rose through the ranks and, in a short time, became one of the lord's inner circle of retainers.

This lord had a daughter, a selfish, pampered woman. *If I marry her,* thought the samurai, *my fortune will be secured.*

So, coldheartedly, he courted and won her. The wedding was a grand and solemn affair. Then all went on as before. His wife sat before the mirror plucking her brows and trying on an endless array of costly robes while her husband, the samurai, attended his lord and vied for honors on the field with bow, spear, and sword. The samurai also now accompanied his wife as she was carried in her litter from shop to shop to purchase cloth, robes, trinkets, and jewels. Standing in the street beside the litter-bearers, his heart began to chafe at the vanity and banality of it all. He took no joy in the life of riches he had finally gained.

He began to dream of his first wife. At night he would see her beautiful face, her tender eyes bright with longing for him, her long black hair flowing over her shoulders. He would hear again the *clack clack* of her loom as she wove the beautiful cloth. He would reach for her and awake to look with dismay and disgust on all around him.

After a time the dreams came to him even in daylight. As he waited while his new wife bought her endless array of things, the face of his first wife would rise before him. Her smile, her fine face, her delicate hands, her long black hair. Over and over these images came to him, flooding him with longing and with love. At night bitter tears filled his eyes. He now knew himself to be no success, but rather, a fool. He had cast aside the woman who had loved him, whom he had loved, to accumulate mere wealth and power. As he saw this truth he grew determined to leave it all. *I will abandon this life of position and honor and return to my true wife and make amends,* he thought.

One night he mounted his horse and rode away through the darkness toward the city of Kyoto. After days of hard riding he entered the city near midnight. The streets were dark, deserted as a tomb as, heart pounding, he approached his old home. He rode into the courtyard. The weeds were tall. In the moonlight he could see that the paper of the sliding *shoji* screens had been torn in places. *It has not been easy for her,* he thought sadly. *But now I am back and shall make it all up to her. Yes. All will be well.*

He tied his horse, went up on the veranda, removed his sandals, slid the door back, and entered. He walked from room to room. Then he heard it, a quiet *clack clack*—the sound of someone working at a loom. His heart leapt with anticipation. He slid back a final door. There she sat at the great loom, her back to him. Her robe was patched. Her beautiful black hair cascaded over her thin shoulders and down her back.

She turned and she saw him. And a radiant smile blossomed on her beautiful, wan face. She rushed to him and he gathered her into his arms. "Forgive me," he wept. "Forgive me. I have been a fool. I will make it up to you. I swear it."

"Hush," she whispered through her tears. "Hush. What does that matter now? My prayers have been answered. You have returned. Come. Come."

They spent the night together talking, laughing and crying, holding each other through the hours of darkness as the candles burned low and, at last, guttered out. The samurai drifted off to sleep.

He awoke to morning light falling full upon his face. He opened his eyes. The sun was shining in directly upon him. How could this be? He sat up and saw that a great section of the roof had long ago caved in from rot. He rubbed his eyes, but it was no dream. The sun in the sky overhead still shone down upon him. Bewildered, he looked around.

Mildew glistened on torn paper walls and fallen beams. Weeds grew through rotted flooring. A broken loom stood in the center of the room. His wife lay beside him, her back to him, her thin shoulders draped in the patched kimono, her long black hair flowing down her back and onto the floor. He took hold of her, turned her toward him, and . . . it was a skeleton that lay beside him. Long, long ago his gentle wife had died of grief, of loneliness, and of longing.

STORY NOTES

Urashima Taro

"Urashima Taro," perhaps Japan's favorite folktale, exists in numerous versions. It was the personal favorite of Lafcadio Hearn, who based his telling on a literary text almost fifteen hundred years old. His version appears in *Out of the East: Reveries and Studies in New Japan*. It is so popular that in the Ura shrine in the town of Ine, near the coast, a lacquered box said to be the one given to Urashima Taro by the princess is on display to this day.

Like "Rip Van Winkle," this story reveals the relativity of time, which can seem to move fast or slow. William Butler Yeats's long poem *The Wanderings of Oisin*, a retelling of an old Irish legend, bears an uncanny resemblance to "Urashima Taro."

Green Willow

When Hearn first arrived in Japan in 1890 he wrote:

> Why should trees be so lovely in Japan? . . . Is it that the trees have so long been domesticated and caressed by man in this land of the Gods, that they have acquired souls, and strive to show their gratitude . . . by making themselves more beautiful for man's sake? Assuredly they have won men's hearts by their loveliness . . . that is to say, Japanese hearts. Apparently there have been some foreign tourists of the brutal class . . . since it has been deemed necessary to set up inscriptions in English announcing that "it is forbidden to injure the trees."
>
> [*Wandering Ghost*]

Hearn's version, in his collection *Kwaidan,* has some confusions and it has some differences from this retelling. These include a pardon by a kind prince, and an ending which closes the story with Tomotada's prayers. I let the growing cycle of death and renewal, appropriate to trees, carry the story further.

As a child I spent many happy hours in treetops. Trees were my friends and companions. Trees, of course, freely give us life-sustaining oxygen. Without them and other plants, there could be no life on earth. Might not this great gift be considered a kind of love? I find stories like "Green Willow" and "The Pine of Akoya" important today, when so many forests are in danger. These tales help reconnect us with our own perhaps temporarily forgotten love for our benefactors, the trees.

Ho-ichi the Earless

The story, "Mimi-Nashi Ho-ichi" as it is called in Japanese, is based on actual events. In 1185 the Heike and Genji clans came together in a final confrontation; in which the Heike lost control of Japan forever. Blind *biwa* players (a *biwa* is an instrument somewhat like a lute), of which Ho-ichi is one, were trained from childhood to recount the entire epic story. The crabs mentioned at the beginning are known even today as Heike crabs and are said to be the spirits of the dead Heike samurai.

"Ho-ichi the Earless" was my daughter's favorite at age five. Perhaps this was because the title character, though frail, blind, and alone, ultimately triumphs over terrible odds. The story's final message is one of hope. The words painted on Ho-ichi's body were probably the text of the Heart Sutra, or *Hannya Shingyo (Heart of Perfect Wisdom).* Its key line is, "Form is only Emptiness, Emptiness is only form."

My retelling, based on Hearn's in *Kwaidan,* was influenced also by the gorgeous and chilling film *Kwaidan,* directed by Masaki Kobayashi, and by the beautiful cut-paper illustrations by Masakuzu Kuwata in *Earless Ho-ichi: A Classic Japanese Tale of Mystery.*

The Snow Woman

My version is based on Lafcadio Hearn's "Yuki-Onna," a retelling of a story a Japanese farmer told him, which can be found in Hearn's *Kwaidan, Stories and Studies of Strange Things (kwaidan* means "weird tales"). Most of the stories in that collection were adapted from tales Hearn found in old Japanese books.

I wanted to bring out something that Hearn bypassed—a feeling of tenderness. The Snow Woman in the end acts mercifully and spares her husband, who violated the condition of silence she placed on him. It is her willingness to suffer rather than do harm that turns the story into a thing of beauty. Mercy wins out over the demands of justice. One original detail that emerged during the course of my years of telling the tale is her icicle-like teeth—chilling and, I think, neat.

Kogi

"The Story of Kogi the Priest" is the title Hearn used, but the tenth-century source has another, "The Carp That Came to My Dream." That tale was my source and may have been Hearn's as well. I found the story in *Ugetsu Monogatari (Tales of Moonlight and Rain)* an eighteenth-century collection by Ueda Akinari.

It is said that in the ninth century a Buddhist priest by the name of Kogi actually lived at a temple on the shores of Lake Biwa, the setting for this tale. Whether true or not, the story gives reality to our wishes, visions, and dreams.

In my retelling, besides developing the underwater scenes—which was great fun—I changed the order of the events. Now we can experience Kogi's dream as it occurs, rather than hearing about it after he awakes.

The Crane Maiden

Tales of the graceful change of a woman into a swan or crane are very ancient. In Europe, images of The Goddess as a swan or crane have been dated as far back as the Upper Paleolithic, or almost 25,000 years ago. Perhaps there is some memory of these myths in our nursery-rhyme figure Mother Goose.

In this elegant and tender tale, the crane maiden returns to her own realm and the old couple remain human beings. Yet a relationship of love and gratitude now exists. This emphasis on tenderness and intimacy, rather than on boundary and separation, is often the gift of Japanese tales.

The Pine of Akoya

This beautiful story, a relatively little-known tale of love between a human and tree, is a companion piece to "Green Willow," a better-known tale on the same theme.

The retelling is based on a version in *Folk-Legends of Japan,* by Richard Dorson, which is, in turn, from *Too Ibun (Strange Things Heard from the Eastern Districts of Oshu,* by Kizen Sasaki). As I elaborated on its atmosphere of elegant mystery, to my delight, new details such as the inscribed flute, emblem of a mysterious and undying love, began to emerge.

A Frog's Gift

In a sense, what is unusual about this story is precisely what makes it familiar to Western audiences—the staunch, wise, third daughter; the marriage and happy ending. Japanese tales often close on a less predictable, more suggestive note. The appearance of a wise animal/crone and the basic theme of the tale—one good turn deserves another—also make it accessible.

A bare-bones version of this little known story appears in *Ancient Tales in Modern Japan* and was the basis for my retelling. Readers interested in seeing how stories grow and change might want to compare these two versions. The hissing voice of the warrior, the scale-like glittering of the armor, the musical croaking of the frogs, the dress the color of rice fields or frog skin, the old lady's "wide" mouth, large round eyes, hoarse voice and hopping step are just some of the details that emerged in my telling.

The Boy Who Drew Cats

Here is a classic Japanese ghostly tale. It's eerie, mysterious, and full of deep meaning. I love the child's faith in the promptings of his imagination and talent, and that in the end these are the things that save not only him but everyone. I love, too, the mystery of his drawings coming to life. The pairing of the old wise man (the priest) and the divine or talented child is archetypal.

This version, clearly based on Hearn's, was shaped by my many years of actually *telling* the tale. Details emerged in this process which encouraged me to continue, like the boy, in trusting my own imagination. *The Boy Who Drew Cats* was one of the first stories I ever told.

Black Hair

While it is brief, this is a complex love story, a good ghost tale, and also a moral one. Yet we wish the samurai's wife didn't have to suffer so.

I first came across this story almost thirty years ago. In my retelling, I focused on its implicit moral pattern, a negative demonstration of the Golden Rule—Do unto others as you would have them do unto you—and on the sorrow of the samurai's terrible failure, rather than on any sense of horror or terror.

Akinari, Ueda. *Ugetsu Monogatari: Tales of Moonlight and Rain*. Tokyo: Charles E. Tuttle Company, 1977.

Blyth, R. H. *Haiku*. 4 vols. Tokyo: Hokuseido Press, 1949, 1950, 1952.

Cott, Jonathan. *Wandering Ghost: The Odyssey of Lafcadio Hearn*. New York: Kodansha International, 1992.

Dorson, Richard. *Folk Legends of Japan*. Rutland, VT: Charles E. Tuttle Co., 1962.

Hearn, Lafcadio. *The Boy Who Drew Cats and Other Tales of Lafcadio Hearn*. New York: Macmillan, 1963.

———. *Earless Ho-ichi*. Tokyo: Kodansha International Ltd., 1966.

———. *In Ghostly Japan*. Rutland, VT: Charles E. Tuttle Co., 1971.

———. *Kwaidan*. Rutland, VT: Charles E. Tuttle Co., 1971.

Henderson, Harold G., ed. *Tales from the Japanese Storytellers*. Collected by Post Wheeler. Rutland, VT: Charles E. Tuttle Co., 1976.

Kawai, Hayao. *The Japanese Psyche*. Dallas, TX: Spring Publications, 1982.

Kitagawa, Hiroshi, and Tsuchida, Bruce T. *The Tale of the Heike*. Tokyo: University of Tokyo Press, 1977.

Martin, Rafe. *Ghostly Tales of Japan,* (audio cassette). Cambridge, MA: Yellow Moon Press, 1989.

———. *The Hungry Tigress: Buddhist Legends and Jataka Tales*. Cambridge, MA: Yellow Moon Press, 1995.

Mayer, Fanny Hagin. *Ancient Tales In Modern Japan*. Bloomington, Indiana: Indiana University Press, 1984.

Pound, Ezra, ed. *The Classic Noh Theater of Japan*. New York: New Directions Publishing Corp., 1959.

Sakade, Florence. *Japanese Children's Favorite Stories*. Rutland, VT: Charles E. Tuttle Co., 1958.

———. *Japanese Children's Stories*. Rutland, VT: Charles E. Tuttle Co., 1959.

Sazanami, Iwaya. *Japanese Fairy Tales*. Tokyo: Hokuseido, 1936.

Waley, Arthur. *The Noh Plays of Japan*. Rutland, VT: Charles E. Tuttle Co., 1976.

Yasuda, Yuri. *Old Tales of Japan*. Tokyo: Charles E. Tuttle Co., 1956.